ECHO

JOHN URBANCIK

ERASERHEAD PRESS
PORTLAND, OREGON

ECHO

ECHO

Echo is just the beginning of the Secret History of the Palace Theater. I will return to those halls, and I hope you'll return with me. There's magic to be found there.

I wrote this portion of the Palace Theater in Richmond, Virginia. Though I doubt you can see that city in these pages, I see the high ceiling of my apartment there, which echoed everything back to us. I feel the winter cold after having spent so much time in Florida even when the story doesn't invoke it. Memories are strong and can often invoke times and places specific to your experience of the story.

The times in which these tales were written were still good. But nothing lasts forever.

ACKNOWLEDGMENTS

I wrote this while living in Richmond, Virginia, and must thank Brent Tiano for all of his help and support then as well as Mary Lescher, without whom a great many of my stories might never have been told.

I must also thank Morgan, who has walked with me through the darkness.

Thank you Rose, and everyone at Eraserhead, for seeing promise in the absurd.

As always, a special thanks to Sabine and the Rose Fairy.

ONE

Maybe it was lightning: a stray thunderbolt let loose by the gods. Or an errant wish gone wrong; radiation; cosmic activity or seismic activity or occult activity. Poisonous gases. An uncontrolled radical particle, an ionized electron, a fluctuation in the magnetic field. Maybe the convergence of a rotten anti-inflammatory after a preternatural headache and something more sinister, perhaps Scarlet, on the other side. Maybe it was just because they looked into the same mirror at the same time and noticed the same crack. Maybe it was bad magic.

Whatever the reason, they switched.

They switched, and Nicholas found himself in a place both utterly familiar and completely bizarre. The walls were where his walls had always been. The old apartment was his, but the color was gone. In its place, the walls were blacks and whites, black like charcoal and white like chalk. Everything in the room, the desk and tables, the chairs, the lamps, all sketched in variations of these. The bulb glowing on the lamp gave off a bright, distinct white light, more substantive than should be, thicker, cleaner.

First thing, Nicholas went into the bedroom and changed clothes. Out of the jeans, out of the tee shirt, into something more likely to provide camouflage this side of the mirror. Coal jeans, chalk shirt, coal jacket. The streets were his streets, though the color was different. The cars were the same shapes he'd left behind. The sidewalk was just as cracked, the buildings just as old and crumbly. The Nicholas on this side of the mirror had done no better for himself than he had. The apartment was a hole, the neighborhood bordered on ruin, and the sound of passing subways shook the world.

The people on this side of the mirror were painted with the same dust as the rest of the world. That would take some getting used to. He wasn't sure how long he'd be here. What if it was a permanent switch?

He explored the neighborhood and found the same deli at the corner. Inside, it was the same clerk, or a variation of him. Nicholas had never learned his name. The guy looked up. "Hey, Nicholas," he said, tilting his head in a funny way. "You don't look well. You need something to make you better?"

"Always."

"I got just the thing." The clerk called back to someone in the kitchen. "Hey, Jerry, guess who's dropped in for your pastrami."

A big guy emerged, Jerry, wiping his hands on a towel, but he stopped, froze entirely, the moment he saw Nicholas. His eyes narrowed. "You."

Nicholas hesitated. What had his mirror self done?

Jerry threw the rag and ran around the side of the counter. Nicholas didn't wait. He fled. Out the door, down the street, toward an alley. Jerry was big and slow, but Nicholas was no Olympic runner, speed or distance. He turned left, then right, then bumped off the side of a chain link fence.

It was hard to run through all the blacks and whites. The lack of color, the sketchiness of everything that was visible, played with his sense of depth. He crashed into a set of garbage cans. He ran like a drunk man, a madman, a freak.

"I'll kill you!" Jerry kept yelling behind him. It wasn't the welcome he had hoped for. Around another corner, he ran into a wall.

So the geography wasn't exactly identical.

Jerry caught him, got a fist around his throat, foam spraying from his mouth as he snarled. "We thought you'd learned," Jerry said, bringing a fist back to throw a punch. But he hesitated. "What the hell's wrong with your face?"

Nicholas grinned, but the grip around his windpipe did not let up. He tried to say something, cough something, draw any breath at all. He kicked, maybe caught a shin, maybe didn't manage to catch anything. He tried to punch. He'd never been a fighter. Didn't learn until college not to keep his thumb tucked inside his fist. Hitting Jerry was like hitting slabs of meat. He quite suddenly understood Rocky.

Jerry forced him backwards, against the wall, cracking Nicholas's head against the bricks. Nicholas was able to breathe again, at least a breath, and that was all he needed. "Disease," he said, gasping, not needing to exaggerate the sound of it. "Terminal."

Jerry flinched, let go, stepped back. "What do you mean, disease?"

"I'm dying," Nicholas said, staring into the pasty white face of the big man. "Days, maybe a week. It's highly contagious." Every word increased the concern in Jerry's expression.

"I don't believe you."

"It's terminal."

"They'd have you locked up," Jerry said. "Quarantined."

"I escaped," Nicholas said. He stepped forward. "To find you."

"You're crazy," Jerry said.

Nicholas grinned. "Yes." He touched the back of his head. There was blood. Red. Brilliant and bright on this scratched side of the mirror. Jerry's eyes went wide. There wasn't much blood, but it was the most vivid color he'd ever seen. Nicholas shoved the fingers forward. "See?" he said. "I'm a walking deathtrap."

"I don't know what you are," Jerry said, "but I'll be glad when you're dead." He walked away, dignity intact, straight and tall and satisfied, a man who'd meant to kill and did so. Nicholas, meanwhile, struggled not to hyperventilate. When the big man was out of sight, he bent over double, coughed, wiped his brow, felt the back of his head again. He looked back at the brick wall behind him. A smear of red.

In a nearby open window, a white cat, staring at him, swished its tail and licked its paw.

ONE

Maybe it was lightning: a stray thunderbolt let loose by the gods. Or an errant wish gone wrong; radiation; cosmic activity or seismic activity or occult activity. Poisonous gases. An uncontrolled radical particle, an ionized electron, a fluctuation in the magnetic field. Maybe the convergence of a rotten anti-inflammatory after a preternatural headache and something more sinister, perhaps Scarlet, on the other side. Maybe it was just because they looked into the same mirror at the same time and noticed the same crack. Maybe it was bad magic.

Whatever the reason, they switched.

They switched, and Nicholas found himself in a place both utterly familiar and completely bizarre. The walls were where his walls had always been. The old apartment was his, but the colors were changed. In its place, the walls were sick with color, lurid, nearly overwhelming. The bulb glowing on the lamp gave off a pale, dirty variation of light.

First thing, Nicholas went through the apartment, pocketing anything he thought might be useful or valuable—cash in a funny hue but with the same Presidential portraits, a ring that might be gold, a pocketknife. A jacket. There wasn't much. The Nicholas on this side of the mirror hadn't done any better in life than he had. Outside, the neighborhood was the same, if garish, but he was getting used to that. The sidewalk was just as cracked, the buildings just as old and crumbly. The colors of the people would take some getting used to. What if it was a permanent switch?

He explored the neighborhood. The same deli at the corner. He thought about going in, demanding pastrami on rye, just to test the stock of the people on this side of the mirror, and then went in, nodded to the clerk as if everything was normal.

"Hey, Nicholas," they guy said, tilting his head in a funny way. "You don't look well. You need something to make you better?"

Nicholas grinned. "Always."

"I got just the thing." The clerk called back to the kitchen. "Hey, Jerry, we got any of your momma's soup left?"

A big guy emerged, Jerry, wiping his hands on a towel. His eyes reached Nicholas, eyes full of color, and he said, "Yeah, I think so."

"I bet you do," Nicholas said, thinking how easily a man could slip a bit of cyanide into soup and watch their enemies choke and gasp and die. "Not today, thanks. I've got other plans."

"You don't look right," Jerry said. "Pale. Pasty."

"Yeah, I'm sick," Nicholas said. "Diseased and dying. Probably it's contagious as all hell. You'll probably want to burn this place down after I'm gone."

He left with an apple. A solid, real apple he'd slipped into his jacket pocket. He wondered how something so red must taste. He tossed it once as he walked away from the deli, then took a bite. There was so much juice, it spilled over his lip and down his chin, and it was damn sweet.

"I could definitely like this place," Nicholas said to no one, and took another bite.

He wondered how the Lissa on this side of the mirror would respond to him.

In a window as he passed, a black cat, staring at him, swished its tail and licked its paw.

TWO

Before he reached Lissa's apartment, Nicholas stopped outside the Palace Theater. On his side of the mirror, it was a crappy, rundown place closed years ago. Here, it maintained all that crappy rundown appeal, but it hadn't been closed. There were posters in both spots, one for some sort of choir and the other for a magician. The name wasn't written in very big letters, and the face wasn't clear, but he had stared at that face in the mirror's reflection for the entirety of his life.

"I'm a fucking magician?" he said aloud. Even with the colored face, and all those gaudy reds and golds, no one could hide his own face from him, not even the backwards face from the other side. He stared for a moment, leaned closer to get a better look. The assistant, pictured even smaller—was that Lissa? Impossible.

He knocked on the window for the ticket seller. Though no one was immediately visible, through that door someone might be working. When no one answered, he tried the front door. Locked.

He let himself in anyhow.

The lobby was as wide as the building but not very deep, and there was a stand for selling assorted candies and sodas. He couldn't read the names because the cacophony of color blinded him. He walked through the doors into the theater itself, at the far end of the rightmost aisle. There was a mirror, one of those standalone types you could move from house to house and spin around until it shattered, on the stage. What would be the point? There was also a box of some sort, and a bag full of stuff, but he didn't get closer to investigate.

According to the poster, the show started at 8. Hours from now. What would happen when their precious little illusionist failed to show up and make with the tricks?

He exited the way he'd come in, not bothering to lock the door as he left, and headed for Lissa's apartment. Now, he absolutely had to see her. She lived on the third story of a walkup just a few blocks away—on both his side of the mirror and here. He saw her name on the mailboxes, pressed the buzzer, waited for her voice over the loudspeaker. It sounded no better here than on his side. "I'm not expecting anyone."

"Nicholas," he said, answering the unanswered question. He wondered, briefly, if his voice sounded the same on both sides, but apparently it was enough. She buzzed him in.

She wasn't waiting in the hall when he reached the third floor. When he turned the knob, it was locked. He knocked. No use in picking it if she expected him. After a moment, she opened the door only as far as the chain would allow.

"Lissa," he said.

She looked gorgeous, even in full color. He smiled and held out his arms with palms up, essentially asking what was up with the chains.

"Show starts in three hours," she told him. "Call is in two. I'm not ready, and I don't want to see you here."

"What gives?" he asked. "You should be thrilled to see me."

"Is there something wrong with you?" She squinted from behind the door. "You look...dry. Flaky."

He frowned. "I merely wanted to see a familiar face," he said. "A lovely face like yours. A face I see when I close my eyes."

"Have you got a fever?"

"We're a team, you and me," Nicholas said. "Why are you keeping me out?"

"Nicholas," she said, distinctly, enunciating every

word. "We work together. We do. But you've never been to my place alone before, and I don't think now's the time..."

"Now," Nicholas said, "is definitely the time. Obviously, I've wasted enough of it."

She smiled in spite of herself. He was glad to see it. He was on his way to fixing things. Because despite the apple, there were things wrong with his life on this side of the mirror, things horribly awry, and he intended to fix them.

Averting her eyes, she said, "Give me a moment." Then she shut the door.

While waiting, Nicholas looked up and down the hallway, at the rich, shiny woods, the green and white tiles, the yellowish tint to the walls. He could take the colors in muted tones like that. He might even grow to like them.

When Lissa opened the door again , she pointed an Oliveri 9mm at him. From behind the barrel of the gun, she said, "Trust me, this is for the best."

TWO

When fully recovered, Nicholas escaped the alleys and returned to the streets. It was too dark back there, with the streaks of black and spots of white. If he looked at anything in particular for too long, it gave him vertigo.

Nicholas made his way to the streets and did the only thing he really thought he should. He had a show that night. The Palace Theater was only a few blocks away, if he hadn't gotten too disoriented. It took a few minutes to figure out where he was and make his way in the right direction, but when he got there the marquee with his poster in it was empty except for the chalky threads of a spider's web and a good supply of dust. The ticket counter was barren. The doors were not merely locked, but chained shut.

21

He knocked anyway. The echoes bounced back, but obviously no one was inside. He didn't understand. Was there another stage somewhere else?

Lissa would know.

He'd been to her apartment only a few times, for parties and such, and he didn't know if he could find his way back. The city sounded the same. People on the streets ignored him, mostly, though one or two nodded in acknowledgement of another human being. Their faces were either black or white, the same as everything else in this world. It was beginning to be unnerving.

He found Lissa's apartment, climbed the stoop, and pressed the button. After a moment, she buzzed him in, no questions asked. She lived at the top of a three story walkup. He climbed through the darkness and found her door standing open.

He stopped at the threshold and knocked on the open door. "Lissa?" he called. When she didn't answer, he looked around the side of the door and called her name again. The door opened onto the kitchen at one end of the tenement. Next was a living room, where Lissa sat wearing a sleek black dress with a high slit. Her legs were crossed, her lips twisted into a rictus smile. She pointed a 9mm Oliveri at him. From behind the barrel of the gun, she said, "Trust me, this is for the best."

THREE

Nicholas held up his empty hands. "Isn't that a bit of an overreaction?" He didn't back away. If she meant to shoot him, she'd have to risk getting splattered by blood. Murder was always a messy business.

"Back away," she said, "and never come back here."

"What'd I do?" Nicholas asked. It was a stupid question. She wasn't going to tell him.

Lissa gestured with the gun. "I want to see you outside and walking away inside sixty seconds," she said. She didn't issue any further threat. She didn't have to.

"I didn't mean anything by it," Nicholas said. "I was just thinking...I mean, I didn't want to lose you."

"I was never yours to lose."

"Which is the same as losing you," Nicholas said.

When she didn't immediately respond, he added, "You're beautiful, Lissa, you always have been, and I've been a fool not to see it before. Look at me now, here, risking my life to tell you this."

"I quit," she told him.

"One more show," he said. "Please."

She eyed him, still from behind the gun. Her aim was steady. Her eyes steady. She said, "I have a headache."

"One more show," he said. He didn't even know what a show would entail. Probably magic. Illusion. Lissa stepping into a box and disappearing. He must've been to a magic show at some point in his life. What should he expect?

"You," she said, "promised me real magic."

"I did?"

"Said you'd make me a star."

"I must've been drinking."

"You," she said, "don't do a damn thing on that stage. I do all the work. I do it."

"I understand, I do."

"I've wanted to quit for a while now," she said. "I've wanted to shoot you for almost as long."

"Well, you've already done one," Nicholas said. "Just one more show, and I'm sure we can work things out."

"You don't know how to work things out. Did you see your audience last night? Did you see it? Thirteen people. Thirteen, Nicholas, and three of them didn't even pay for a ticket. You know what my share of that is?"

"Insufficient, I'm sure."

"Ten dollars."

"No one can live on ten dollars a night," Nicholas said. "And how much did you make?"

Nicholas shook his head. "I honestly don't know."

"No fortune, I can tell you that much," Lissa said. She gestured with the gun again. "Go. Go, or I swear to every god you've ever known, I'll pull this trigger."

Nicholas didn't turn. He didn't want to give her his back. He'd rather see the bullet coming when it did. He backed toward the stairs, took the first step carefully, then said, "After the show tonight, Lissa, I'll make everything right. I swear it."

She said nothing. If anything, her trigger finger tensed. Nicholas hopped down the stairs. Once he started moving, he ran, taking the steps three and four at a time. If something broke inside her, if Lissa came out after him, he'd already be out of range. He spun around at the landing and went down the next flight, down until he was out the front door, on the street again, with all its overwhelming colors. He felt lightheaded. He glanced up at Lissa's silhouette in the window.

Long shadows stretched across the street, swallowing some of the vibrancy of everything. He went in a random direction, not sure where he'd go next. He had no real desire to put on a magic show.

The only tricks he knew involved lifting wallets and watches and fancy gold-tipped pens. However, if he was some sort of illusionist on this side of the mirror, maybe it was time to work some real magic.

THREE

Nicholas held up his hands, showing empty palms. "Whatever you think I did, I didn't," he said. "Honest." He didn't back away. If she meant to shoot him, he'd never get back out to the hallway in time.

"Closer," she said, gesturing with the gun. "I never expected to see you again."

"I'm not who you think I am," he said.

"I suppose not. An escape artist as well as a thief?" She grinned. It was a carnivorous grin. He didn't like it. This was not the Lissa he knew.

"Something happened," he said. "I'm on the wrong side of..."

Lissa gestured with the gun again. "Sit." She flipped the end of the gun, briefly, toward the couch. "I trusted you."

27

Obviously, she expected an answer. Nicholas said, "I don't know what to say."

"You can't talk your way out of this, Nicholas," she said. He didn't like the way his name sounded off her tongue, like that of a pet who had done something wrong. He sat at the edge of the couch like a coiled spring. She rose. Holding the gun at her side, she stepped toward him, making a show of it. "I've let you slide on a lot of things," she said, "because I've always liked you, Nicholas. I've always found you...I'll say attractive, in a not so obvious way." She towered over him now, all black and white and metal. Her finger never left the trigger. "So I asked you to do one simple little thing to make it up to me, Nicholas, and you couldn't manage it, could you?"

"There's still time," Nicholas told her.

"I'm not so sure," she said. "You look...pasty." She made a face to show her disgust. "Like you're coming apart."

"It's not like that."

"Quiet, now," Lissa said, tapping his knee with the barrel of the gun. "I'm talking."

He didn't respond. Even when she seemed to want a response, he didn't. It had been a mistake, going to someone he had known. Everything was different on this side of the mirror. The people he trusted couldn't be trusted. The people he loved would be filled with loathing and contempt. He had seen Star Trek. He should've known what would happen.

"So what," Lissa asked, "are you going to do..." She paused here, leaned close, raised the gun again to point it at his chest. "To make it up to me?"

When he didn't immediately answer, she moved her arm slightly and pulled the trigger. The bullet tore into the couch next to him. She returned her aim to him, narrowed her eyes. He could practically see smoke drifting out of the barrel, though that might've been his imagination. "Only thing I can do," he said, trying to sound like he belonged on this side of the mirror. "I'll make some magic."

She smiled. It was a beautiful smile. The gun took nothing away from that. "Oh?"

"At the theater," Nicholas said. "I can set everything up there." He had no idea what he would set up. He was only trying to buy some time. The longer she waited before shooting him, the more likely he'd survive. When his chance to escape came, he'd take it.

"There's no theater."

"The old Palace Theater."

She seemed to recognize it. "Kinky," she said, winking. Then: "Sure, why not? Lead the way." She swung the gun again like a beckoning finger. He hoped she wouldn't accidentally shoot him.

Outside, long shadows stretched across the street, disguising the starkness of chalk and charcoal, and lights had started to be lit—neon lights, not bright but certainly vibrant. He was in no frame of mind to put on a magic show. However, if he was any sort of an illusionist, it was time to work some real magic.

FOUR

Nicholas ran through an array of possible tricks he could perform. He only needed a distraction. Then he could run. He could worry about a destination when he was on the move. Of course, Jerry had caught him. There was a good chance Lissa, not his assistant Lissa but some otherworldly variation thereof, would catch him too. Catch him and shoot him.

Card and coin tricks seemed out of the question. Rope work might be appropriate, if he could somehow entangle Lissa in it. The only real solution, of course, was either to trap her—but none of his boxes would actually be in the theater—or take the gun.

Nicholas knew as much about guns as he knew about cameras: point and shoot. Hope for the best.

As they walked, the gun wasn't visible. She had it tucked in her bag, at the end of her hand, which still clutched the weapon and pointed it at him. The bullet would go right through the bag if she shot him. So he did nothing to incur her wrath.

The walk to the theater was only a few blocks, but it had been a long day already. Nicholas felt drained, physically and emotionally. And in some other way, too, that he couldn't describe, something to do with being on the wrong side of the mirror.

The theater looked rotten and neglected. The walls were brick, and too thick to break in, but crumbly and dusty. With enough time, a person could dig their way inside. The doors, locked and chained, didn't look like they would easily move under any circumstance. They were heavy, wood and metal, the hinges rusted into place.

Nicholas was beginning to discern differences in the shades of white and black. These were not grays, but variations in thickness and intensity.

And the neon lights confused him. They didn't shine like a sun or a flashlight, but as night fell, more neon blazed. Signs with words, outlines around doors and windows, even the electric lines to traffic signals buzzed. He tried not to spend too much time noticing. But he noticed.

He looked up at the top of the theater. The three

stories were topped with architectural flourishes worthy of movie palaces from the 1920s, but such outcroppings had always been weak and were clearly eroding.

"I am intrigued," Lissa said.

"There's an entrance in the back," Nicholas said.

"These locks too tough for you?" She was teasing him. What was he on this side of the mirror?

"Less conspicuous," he said.

An alley ran alongside the theater. The building was straight and featureless from the alley, completely lacking in extravagance. Also, the side lacked windows, doors, platforms, anything that might allow entry. Nicholas still had no real plan other than delay.

The back doors were as big as the front but plain, thinner wood, without the glamour that faced the public. The chains were not as thick. And there was a window. With some effort, Nicholas pushed the window open. He would've broken it if necessary, but this seemed better.

"I'm almost impressed," Lissa said. "Too bad you couldn't put your talents to better use for me."

"Everything," Nicholas said, climbing through the window, "is for you." It was a tight squeeze, but he made it inside. Lissa squirmed through even more easily, making quite a show of it in that silky black dress. Together, they crept through the darkness behind the stage.

The green room door stood open, and the room beyond looked empty. The various set pieces, whether being stored or in use, were gone, though a couple of unrecognizable backdrops had apparently been too large to remove. There were sandbags and lighting rigs and a few chairs scattered around. They passed through the curtain onto the stage.

It was so dark, Nicholas could see nothing. The stage, the auditorium, all the seats—if they were still there—were swallowed by darkness. Lissa held him by the shoulder, her grip firm, not out of fear but to keep him from running.

With a heavy thud, a spotlight came on. It caught the two of them on the stage. A voice from faraway, perhaps the balcony, perhaps aiming the light at them, said, "Welcome to my Palace Theater."

FOUR

Nicholas went back to the theater. Not intentionally. That was just the direction his feet took him. He stared at his face in the poster. The face that stared back at him from the mirror. As night fell, the color seeped away, making it almost exactly like him.

And this, he realized, would be his greatest theft. Not merely cash, but a whole life. The Nicholas on this side of the mirror lived differently than he did. He would claim that as his own, even if it meant performing tricks on a stage. He would find a way to make that work, then twist this whole world to his will.

He entered the theater. Old and even in disrepair, it was not the wreck that he remembered. There was still no one around. The show didn't start for hours. How did a magician prepare for his act?

He probably started by learning what the act was.

He needed Lissa for that. Or a videotape.

He strode into the auditorium, down the aisle between plush red seats, and climbed onto the stage. He pointedly did not look at the mirror. It seemed somehow wrong. He didn't even know why it was on the stage. Approaching it sideways, he pushed it toward an angle so he wouldn't accidentally catch his reflection.

He didn't want to know what his reflection was doing.

Backstage, still he found no one. He passed various props and set pieces for a variety of productions, some of which he might've recognized if they were named. He walked into the green room, which wasn't green at all, where there were trunks and a suitcase and a rack of clothes—suits for the magician. A second, adjoining room had outfits for the assistant, for this side's Lissa— outfits which were impossibly small.

She'd said she did most of the work. But she also wasn't likely to show up tonight. Maybe a better plan was to steal this Nicholas's life and run away with it, maybe to Vegas, and put his skills to work. He could clean up in a town like that. All those drunk tourists throwing cash at the roulette wheel and blackjack tables. He could deal. He had the skills.

He went through the contents of both rooms searching for books with instructions. But of course there weren't any. It was all sleight of hand, right? He could manage that. He couldn't settle on a course of action.

Eventually, he realized he was being watched. He looked up. "Lissa."

She stood in the doorway, arms crossed. "I need more money," she said.

"I can do that."

"I need some now. Today. This moment."

Nicholas pulled the cash he'd taken from, ostensibly, his own apartment. In the low lighting, the green almost looked normal. He had never counted it, and didn't now. "Everything I've got," he said.

She took it. She did count it. She did not seem impressed.

"I can do better," he said. "I have a plan."

The lights went out.

He didn't think Lissa had arranged it, but he didn't want to take any chances. He rushed her, grabbed her, covered her mouth, whispered in her ear. "You still have that gun?"

She struggled, but only for a moment. She nodded. "Where?"

She didn't answer.

With one hand, he took her bag. Though small, it was just large enough to hold a 9mm, and certainly heavy enough. He didn't have a lot of experience with guns. It wasn't part of his line. But he could point. He could shoot. How difficult did it have to be?

Still whispering, he asked, "Are you alone?"

She nodded again. Effectively a lie, since she was with him, but they both knew that wasn't what he meant.

"If I let go," he said, "you have to be quiet."

She nodded.

He let go. She slapped him. Hard. Not quietly at all.

"Fine," he said. "I deserved that. Now quiet." He crept out of the green room. The backstage area was dark and shadowy with only the red light of an exit sign. He went toward the stage, Lissa immediately behind him and holding his shoulder. On stage, he bumped into something, a crate, some part of the act. It was so dark, Nicholas could see nothing. The stage, the auditorium, all the seats were swallowed by darkness.

With a heavy thud, a spotlight came on. It caught the two of them on stage. A voice from faraway, perhaps the balcony, perhaps aiming the light at them, said, "Welcome to my Palace Theater."

FIVE

Trapped by the circle of light, Nicholas—and also Lissa, he assumed—stared defiantly at its source. "You might," Lissa said, "come down here and introduce yourself properly."

To that, the response was laughter. Good, hearty, from the belly laughter.

"I don't like the sound of that," Nicholas said.

"You're a brazen one, I'll give you that," the voice said. It seemed to echo from everywhere at once, as though it owned or was possessed by the theater itself.

Pinpoints of light emerged from the darkness. Eyes. Crouching low and hanging from the rafters and crawling on the walls, all at once a hundred dog-like creatures turned their attention to the stage—and to

Nicholas and Lissa upon it.

"Now," the voice said, "would be a good time to run." Then he laughed again, the maniacal laugh of a madman, and Nicholas found himself entirely in agreement.

Nicholas retreated off stage, Lissa immediately behind him. The creatures chittered behind them, and above them, and alongside them; and the creatures smacked their claws against the walls and floors and ceilings; and one of the creatures howled.

Lissa, even in that dress, leapt straight out the window, feet first, landing perfectly on the uneven broken alley floor in heels. Nicholas caught himself, almost didn't make it out at all, nearly landed flat on his face.

The face that appeared in the window behind them snarled and slavered and showed teeth like spikes, and its eyes burned neon red. Lissa and Nicholas ran. It didn't matter where they went, it only mattered that they got away. They turned random corners, they drove deeper into the labyrinthine alleys into the center of this city.

It was not the city he thought it was.

Eventually, he couldn't run anymore. Lissa dragged him forward. When they stopped, they hadn't escaped anything. They'd been let go. Lissa wasn't even out of breath.

"They're after you, not me," she said.

"How do you figure?"

"The same red eyes."

"My eyes aren't red." He shook his head. With so little color to reference, maybe she mistook brown for red. The neon lights here were not brighter, but they buzzed more loudly, and there were more of them. He didn't know where they were. He recognized none of the buildings, none of the alleys they'd raced through, not even this version of Lissa.

When he'd caught his breath, or at least thought he'd been panting long enough, he managed to stand. Lissa looked at him, into him, examining and appraising him. If she'd been as afraid as he'd been, she hid it exceptionally well.

"Now what?" he asked.

She kissed him. Hard and rough and fast. It was over before he knew it had started. She grinned, all mischief, and said, "I have no idea where we are."

Nicholas looked around. Nothing made sense. The slashes of white and black, the powdery look of everything, the lines of the buildings, the lines of colored light. The disorientation threatened him with dizziness and nausea. He focused instead on Lissa, who had smeared her black lipstick on his lips.

That wasn't focusing.

"It's too dark," Nicholas said. Even in daylight, it was too dark, but she sun had gone and left them somewhere else. He tightened his fists. He said something, he wasn't even sure what, a word or two from an ancient language he'd never known, and created a ball of light out of nothing.

FIVE

Trapped by the circle of light, Nicholas—and also Lissa, he assumed—stared defiantly at the source of that light. "You might," he said, "want to come down here and introduce yourself properly."

To that, the response was laughter. Good, hearty, from the belly laughter.

"I don't like the sound of that," Lissa said.

"You're a brazen one, I'll give you that," the voice said. It seemed to echo from everywhere at once, as though it owned or was possessed by the theater itself.

Pinpoints of light emerged from the darkness. Eyes. Crouching low and hanging from the rafters and crawling on the walls, all at once a hundred dog-like creatures turned their attention to the stage, and to

Nicholas and Lissa upon it.

"Now," the voice said, "would be a good time to run." Then he laughed again, the maniacal laugh of a madman, and Nicholas found himself entirely in agreement.

Nicholas retreated off stage, Lissa immediately ahead of him. The creatures chittered behind them, and above them, and alongside them; and the creatures smacked their claws against the walls and floors and ceilings; and one of the creatures howled.

Nicholas tried to dive straight out the window. It wasn't pretty. He caught himself, twisted in midair, and landed hard on his shoulder. Lissa managed the window with an acrobat's grace.

The face that appeared in the window behind them snarled and slavered and showed teeth like spikes, and its red eyes burned. Nicholas and Lissa ran. It didn't matter where they went, it only mattered that they got away. They turned random corners, they drove deeper into the labyrinthine alleys in the center of this city.

It was not the city he thought it was.

When he thought they weren't being followed anymore—not that they'd gotten away, but that they'd been abandoned—Nicholas stopped running to catch his breath. He slumped against a brick wall. Lissa grinned at him. She didn't even seem to be out of breath. "What were those things?" he asked her.

"They're after you, not me," she said.

"How do you figure?"

"They were the same dusty black you are. With the same red eyes."

"My eyes are not..." He didn't finish, because he didn't really know. The colors here confused him. "If they wanted us," he said, "why the warning? Why tell us to run? Those..." He didn't know what they were. "Those dogs could've ripped us to shreds right there on stage."

He pushed himself back to his feet, away from the wall, and faced Lissa directly. Was she responsible? Had she unleashed this? She stared back at him with genuine fear. Anger, frustration, annoyance, all sorts of other things mixed in there, but definitely fear. He pushed aside the idea that she might be responsible.

"Now what?" she asked.

"I don't know where we are," he admitted. It might've been true on his side of the mirror, as well. Forget the hues and saturation; it was dark enough now, those didn't matter. But the shapes were wrong. The architecture seemed crooked. He wasn't sure how some of these buildings managed to continue standing.

Lissa looked around. "Neither do I." Then she grinned. Pure mischief. "It's too dark," she said, and with a twist of her fingers she created a ball of light out of nothing.

SIX

The ball of light glowed and sizzled. It gave off no heat. It moved when she moved her hands, responding like a marionette might, in ways Nicholas couldn't quite understand. "Impressive."

"I didn't know I could do that."

The ball lit the entire alley. It was a harsh light, and it threw hard shadows. She shifted it and played with it and, after a moment, made it spin.

"And how, exactly, does this help us?" Nicholas asked.

"We can see, for one," Lissa said. She narrowed her eyes at him. "When I told you, months ago, that I could do actual magic, you didn't believe me, did you?"

"You conjured that ball of light from the spirit realm?"

"Something like that."

"What, then?"

"It's tricky," she told him. "Involves math. You wouldn't understand."

He stared at her, but only for a moment. He looked back, toward the theater and the creatures. They didn't seem to be in pursuit anymore.

Lissa tossed the ball into the sky. Over the buildings, it exploded into one and one thousand white sparkles which drifted down and away. She was staring at it and smiling. Briefly, Nicholas did the same. It felt childlike. Naïve. Even innocent. But it felt good, and he liked it, though he didn't think it was a feeling that would last.

As the sparkles scattered and winked out of existence, darkness returned to the alley. Nicholas tried twisting his fingers and saying whatever word it was Lissa might have said, but nothing happened. Lissa, meanwhile, created another, bigger and brighter, ball of light.

"Okay," Nicholas said, "so you're a magician."

"And you," Lissa said, "are an imposter and a fool. What the hell did you think you were doing, anyway?"

"I don't know what you mean."

"You must've tried something, to have sapped all your color. You look positively ghastly, Nicholas." She grinned. "Although I admit, there's a certain appeal to the starkness of you. Are you dying? Did you sign a contract? Did you read something you weren't supposed to read? Dammit, Nicholas, did you at least get the pronunciation right?"

Nicholas was shaking his head to answer her questions. "I have no idea what you're talking about."

"You lie."

"Often," Nicholas admitted, "but not this time."

She regarded him for a moment, seeming to peer right into him. Surely, she realized he wasn't the Nicholas she knew from this side of the mirror. "Apparently," she said, "my magic works better now. It's easier to manipulate." She rolled the ball around her hand like a juggler with a clear glass sphere. "Which means it's stronger, Nicholas, and therefore more dangerous. Less predictable. Volatile, even." She looked as if she blamed him.

"And more fun, I hope," Nicholas said.

"You are exasperating."

Nicholas flashed a grin. "You'd be shocked, how often I hear that."

After a moment of silence, Lissa said, "You're not supposed to be here, right? I mean, you're some other version of the Nicholas I know?"

"You know me, now," Nicholas told her.

"You have to go back."

"I don't think so."

"You brought this trouble with you," Lissa said. "You have to bring it back."

"Oh, no," Nicholas said. "All this is unique to this

side of the mirror." He looked up, at the thick, roiling clouds, gray things that soaked up all the colors and made a sort of soup. "We don't have clouds like that."

"Neither did we."

Nicholas tightened his fists. "Can you magic the weather?" he asked.

"No."

"How do you know?"

"I wouldn't know where to begin," Lissa told him.

"Okay, fine, we'll deal with that later," Nicholas said. "For the moment, we need to break into one of these apartments."

"What?" Lissa blinked. "Why?"

"Those dogs won't be far behind us," Nicholas said. "I for one would feel more comfortable behind the safety of a door."

"Even if it's a door you break open?"

"I've got skills," Nicholas said. "I can do a bit more finesse than breaking open."

"Then we can find a mirror," Lissa said, "and see about switching you back."

"I don't think so."

Lissa smiled. "We'll deal with it later."

"You're forgetting who has the gun here."

"You're forgetting who has all the magic."

Nicholas took a breath, acknowledged—at least inwardly—that he had no idea what the extent of her power might be, and nodded. "Okay, then," he said. "Which way?"

Lissa looked around. She said, "None of this is familiar." She looked back the way they had come, turned to a different direction, and said, "This way."

SIX

The ball of light glowed and sizzled. It gave off no heat. It moved when he moved his hands, responding like a marionette might, in ways he couldn't quite understand.

Lissa stared. "Impressive."

"I didn't know I could do that."

The ball lit the entire alley. It was a harsh light, and it threw hard shadows. He shifted it and played with it and, after a moment, made it spin.

"Do you have any idea what you're doing?"

He caught the ball. Palmed it. Hid it behind his back, which threw his own shadow over Lissa and swallowed this black and white powdery version of her. "None," he admitted, but he smiled. "I mean, I've practiced all sorts of magic, not just illusion, but never with much effect."

"Much effect?"

"A thing here or there, maybe," Nicholas said. He whipped the ball around him, levitated it over his open hand, then sent it into the sky. When it passed the top of the building, it exploded like fireworks, but soundlessly, with a shower of sparkles in every color across the spectrum. He stared up and smiled. Lissa did the same. For a moment, only a moment, he felt like a child discovering all the things.

As the sparkles scattered and winked out of existence, darkness settled again on the alley. This time, with purpose and intention, Nicholas created another ball of light. This was bigger. Brighter. Again, it burned without burning. It radiated no heat whatsoever.

"Maybe my magic works better here, this side of the mirror," Nicholas said. "Maybe it's more likely to work in this world."

Lissa stepped closer, so there was no real space between them. "That might make it more volatile," she said. "Less predictable and more dangerous." Her grin flashed at full intensity. "And more fun."

"So what I have to do," Nicholas said, "is figure out how to return to my side of the mirror."

Lissa frowned. It was exaggerated, but it was honest. "I like this version of you better than mine."

"I don't know what's going on here," Nicholas said.

"Aren't you missing something obvious?"

"What's that?"

"If you came through the mirror, and my version of you went through the mirror, aren't the two of you facing the same problems simultaneously? If you look into a mirror, won't you be there doing the exact same thing?"

Nicholas slumped. All of him, all at once. The logic was terrible and terrifying. "What do you suggest?"

"Verify it."

"Do you happen to have a mirror on you?"

"No."

"Your apartment?"

She shook her head. "I have no idea where that is anymore."

"What do you mean?"

"Look at the sky," Lissa said. There were clouds above the city, thick and roiling, charcoal black clouds reflecting the colors of neon. "It's changed."

Nicholas tightened his fists as he stared. Lissa added, "That's not an ordinary weather system."

"So where do we find a mirror?" Nicholas asked. "And what do I do if..."

"One thing at a time," Lissa said. "Does it have to be a mirror, or just anything reflective?"

"I was working a spell," Nicholas said. "I didn't think it would work, really. I just wanted to peer into the mirror, that's all. But it was definitely a mirror. It's shattered now. Impassable, I would think."

"Any apartment should have a mirror," Lissa said.

"We can just break into any..."

"I'm not a criminal."

"You're a thief, here," she told him. "And a killer, or a would-be killer. You still owe me a body, you know."

"One thing at a time," he told her. "We can knock on someone's door, ask for help."

Lissa laughed. "That might work on your side of the mirror," she said, "but not here."

"No, you're right."

"You just have to open a lock." Lissa grinned again. Put a sexy spin on her voice. "We can knock first, if that makes you feel better."

"I can't pick a lock," Nicholas said.

"Of course you can. You could here, why couldn't you, there?"

"You know, that means we're not identical," Nicholas told her. "On my side, my Lissa is my assistant."

"Assistant?"

"In my magic act."

Lissa laughed, though it was short. "I'll pretend that doesn't hurt me."

Nicholas glanced around. They were at the crossroads of alleys, surrounded by fire escapes and alcoves and garbage bins and windows, but no stoops with doors or doorbells, no true entrances of any sort. "Which way?" he asked.

Lissa looked around, said, "This way," and led Nicholas down an alley they hadn't been running through.

SEVEN

Not far down the alley, Lissa stopped under a fire escape. The ladder had been lowered, so it was a short jump to reach the bottom rung. The ladder was black, the bricks were black, the mortar between the bricks white like chalk, and the sky above a mix of variations on the same. Nicholas couldn't help but see the sky when he looked up. He didn't really want to.

"Here's as good as anywhere," Lissa said. "Start climbing."

"I can't just break through a window."

"It's easier than picking a lock."

She had a point, though it wasn't a good one. "Can't we just find a door?"

"Do you see any doors?"

"At the far end of the alley," Nicholas said. "Surely, that's the street, and all the front doors are there."

"And the back doors are just conveniently missing?" Lissa asked.

Nicholas ignored her. He walked forward. He brought his light with him. Lissa stayed where she was, arms crossed, gun dangling in her hand. "Fine," she said. "I'll wait here."

The alley stretched forever, possibly for miles. Nicholas walked ten minutes without reaching the end of it. The bricks weren't merely the same bricks repeating. Some of the fire escapes were rusted and crumbling. Some of the garbage bins overflowed. White rats scurried in the corners of the shadows, running from his light. Eventually, Nicholas conjured a second, smaller ball of luminescence, reared back like a pitcher, and launched it ahead of him. The ball streaked forward, well faster than he could have thrown it, with a tail like a comet, losing colored flakes of light as it moved.

The ball of light shattered at the end of the alley when it hit a wall. Something ahead groaned, or grumbled, something too far for Nicholas to see.

He sighed. He turned around and started walking, but whatever he'd heard behind him made him run. Nothing chased him. But whatever moved back there, it was large, and briefly there was the sound of wrenching metal.

It didn't take ten minutes to reach Lissa. She stared down at him from the fire escape. "You know you're wearing a dress," Nicholas said.

"And heels," Lissa added. "Get up here."

Nicholas leapt for the ladder. On his first attempt, he missed. He tossed the ball of light up to be level with Lissa, then jumped again. It was a hard climb. He was far from the height of physical perfection. The first few rungs were all upper body strength. Lissa watched, leaning against the railing, and was polite enough not to laugh.

Whatever had made noise behind him sounded closer.

His feet reached the bottom rung, which made the rest of the climb easier.

"There's an open window on the top floor," Lissa said, taking to the stairs.

In total, it was a five story climb, a switchback at every level. The fire escape creaked under their weight, but felt steady. At the top story, they could have climbed higher, to the roof, and that would've been an easier ladder. Lissa slipped into an open window. With a deep breath, Nicholas climbed in after her.

The television screen glowed in a variety of neon colors. If those meant to convey shapes or figures, Nicholas couldn't see them. It was the first thing he noticed in the room. Neon lights lined the corners of the the walls and ceiling in an otherwise white room with black flourishes. A man sat on the couch in front of the screen, so mesmerized he at first didn't notice his visitors until Lissa stepped in front of him and pointed the gun at his face. "We'd like to ask, very politely," she said, "to use a mirror."

"Is that a gun?"

Her trigger finger twitched. "It's not a rolling pin."

The guy looked from Lissa to Nicholas, then back to the gun. "I haven't got no cash."

"Mirror," Nicholas said. "Bathroom, perhaps? Bedroom?"

"Hell, I ain't got the money to buy me one of them reflecting glasses."

Nicholas and Lissa exchanged confused glances.

"Listen," the man said, "there's a guy I know, he can get you a mirror, and some Scarlet pills or something while you're at it. He can do you up real good."

Lissa stepped closer, pressed the barrel against the man's forehead. "That guy you know," she said, "works for me."

"Then why the hell do you come to me looking for a fucking mirror?"

She wanted to pull the trigger. Nicholas could see it. He wanted to, too. He left the living room, walked straight into the kitchen, which was useless, and found a bathroom so small he could fit it in his closet. There was a shower stall, toilet, and sink, and behind the sink a black frame around a wash of white. He tapped it. It might've been glass, but it certainly didn't show anything.

He went to the bedroom. The bedroom was small enough for one, and a woman slept entangled in the sheets. There was a closet, a dresser, an assortment of clothes—nothing fancy—and makeup in shades of black and white—no gray, no neon—but no mirror.

The woman sat up suddenly. She stared straight at Nicholas. "Your eyes," she said.

"My eyes?"

"They're red."

Nicholas wanted to shoot her, too. Instead, he returned to the living room and told Lissa, "They haven't got a mirror."

Lissa frowned. She had stepped away from the guy on the couch and no longer pointed the gun straight at him. "That doesn't make sense."

"I've been trying to tell you," the man said. "Reflections, they ain't easy to find."

"Last one I saw," Lissa said suddenly, though she frowned as she said it, "was on stage at the Palace Theater."

"We just left there," Nicholas said.

"We did."

He didn't add, And that's where the dog things are.

SEVEN

They walked.

They walked and they walked, but the alley stretched infinitely ahead—and possibly infinitely behind. The walls were monochromatic enough, especially in the night, they no longer made Nicholas vertiginous.

Lissa lit the way, and led the way, but there was no place to go. Finally, Nicholas stopped walking. "We're going the wrong way," he said.

"There isn't any other way."

"Up," Nicholas said, looking to the top of the five story building beside them. "Or down." Small windows at foot level indicated basements, maybe basement apartments, and maybe only the top level of multiple basements.

Lissa shook her head. "Not down."

"Fine. Climb."

She hesitated, weighing options. Which was safer, climbing before or after him? She pushed the ball of light into the air. It reached the first level of the fire escape and spun in place. She jumped, caught the bottom of the ladder, and quickly reached the first level. Nicholas shoved the gun into the waistband of his jeans and followed. He kicked as if it would give him momentum. When he reached Lissa, she had split the ball of light into three and was manipulating them around her hand.

"They're surprisingly agile," she said.

"Up," Nicholas said. "To the roof."

They climbed stairs to the top floor, then a ladder to the roof. It was rooftops in all directions, some higher or lower, dotted with vents and shafts and little sheds and air handler units and all manner of unidentifiable machinery, stretching as far into the darkness as Nicholas could say.

"This ain't my city," Nicholas said.

"It's not mine, either," Lissa said. "But I think I can..." She folded the three balls into one again, reared back as if to pitch a baseball, and threw it into the sky. It sizzled and grew and dropped flakes of light as it rose, and it lit the city rooftops.

Essentially, she created a sun, or at least a moon, under the clouds, bright enough to extend their vision a long way. But what they saw—Nicholas saw an endless sea of rooftops. People gathered on some. On others, he saw the dogs, the red-eyed dogs of the theater, creatures he never needed to see with any detail. They were jagged slashes cut from the fabric of reality, black and white and neon and smoke and emerald and crimson, fur sharp like knives, and so many teeth. They sat, alone or in small groups, and every single one of these things, without fail, stared straight back at Nicholas.

And all at once, to the left and to the right, north and south and every other imaginable direction, the dogs—that name was insufficient—got up and started, without hurry, walking in their direction.

"This," Lissa said, "doesn't look good."

"Down," Nicholas said, headed back to the fire escape. Lissa beat him there, and rushed down the ladder. It was like looking into a well; no matter how far he looked, no matter how well he squinted his eyes, the bottom never emerged from the murk. The light of Lissa's little moon slowly faded, but even at full capacity it never stretched that deep into the city canyons. Something moved underneath those shadows. Something swam through the darkness.

As they descended, the darkness rose. Rather than give themselves to whatever hid there, they slipped through an open window on the top story of the building.

The television glowed in a variety of rich, sumptuous colors, none of which Nicholas's eyes were able to translate. If they meant to convey shapes or figure, Nicholas couldn't see them. There was plenty of color in this room, from the deep green blanket to the extraordinarily yellow walls, the bright red toaster in the kitchen, even the purple tee shirt on the man sitting in the couch. He was so mesmerized by what he saw on the screen, he didn't at first notice his visitors until Nicholas stepped in his line of sight and pointed the gun at him. "We need your help."

"Is that a gun?"

Nicholas's trigger finger twitched. "What the hell else would it be?"

The guy looked from Nicholas to Lissa, then back to the gun. "I haven't got no cash."

"Then it's it your lucky day," Nicholas said, "because I ain't looking for any."

"Then what do you want?"

Nicholas didn't actually know. He looked to Lissa. She said, unhelpfully, "A mirror." When no one said anything, she added, "Bathroom, maybe? Or the bedroom."

"I can't say I've got one."

"What do you mean, you haven't got one?" Nicholas asked.

The guy shook his head and scratched his cheek. "I can't say I remember ever looking in a mirror. Dirty frightening things, they are. Who knows who you'll see staring back at you."

Lissa made a noise of frustration and marched into the kitchen, toward the bathroom at the corner of the tenement. Half a minute later, she came back, and walked straight through to the next room, the bedroom.

"Man, your girlfriend's gonna be mad," the guy said to Nicholas.

Nicholas wanted to shoot him. Instead, he looked up when Lissa returned. She said, "They haven't got a mirror."

Nicholas frowned. He lowered the gun. He didn't know what he was doing, and he didn't like not knowing. "That doesn't make sense."

"Why should any of it?" Lissa asked.

"Hey," the guy said suddenly, nearly popping up from the couch, restraining himself only at the last minute when Nicholas raised the gun. "I know where I recognize you from. You're that magician guy, down at the Palace." He smiled. "Hey, that was a great show. Your assistant was gorgeous." He glanced at Lissa. "Hey, that was you, wasn't it?"

She smiled to say yes.

"You're gorgeous," he said.

"This isn't helping," Nicholas said.

"Oh, no, but it is," the guy said. "See, it's like this. Reflections, they ain't easy to find. But the last one I saw, the last time I saw a glass like that, it was on your stage, man. It was part of your show."

"We just left there," Lissa said.

"We did," Nicholas said, but he wasn't happy as he said it. The dogs were everywhere now, but that's where they'd come from.

EIGHT

Into the hall from the apartment, they found long halls with walls slashed white, cheap linoleum, art deco frames every fifty feet, but no pictures, no glass, no mirrors. The doors were labeled, but not with numerals of any sort Nicholas recognized. The symbols were all wrong. Even Lissa frowned at one of those signs before they retreated back to the apartment.

"Yeah," the guy there said. "It looks rather rough out there."

"Can I get you some whiskey or something?" the woman from the bedroom asked.

"No, thanks," Nicholas said.

"Actually," Lissa said, "I could go for a double."

"It doesn't look rough," Nicholas said. "Just different."

"Man, all I've got to do is sit here and watch the

TV. Nothing to concern me, right?"

"There are dogs," Nicholas said. "With eyes like mine. And a temper."

"What do you need?"

The woman returned from the kitchen with whiskey and glasses. She poured for everyone, even Nicholas. He stared at the floor, the cheapest kind of carpet he could imagine, white with flecks of black. He glanced at Lissa. She nodded. Encouragement? He decided to take it. "Okay, I've got this," he said. "I need—a glass. Empty."

Lissa downed hers and handed it over.

"Clean," he said, "and dry."

"Coming right up."

"Fill it with—what kind of herbs have you got?"

"Man, my lady can cook."

The woman smiled shyly. "I can make a thing or two."

"I need some herbs. The more different kinds, the better."

"Sure."

"And from me?" the guy asked.

Nicholas smiled. "We're just getting started. We need a map."

"I ain't got no map."

"Not of this place, you wouldn't," Nicholas said. "I'm trying to make one. Have you got, I don't know, a shirt, a button up shirt, one you'll never need again?"

"That," the guy said, "I've got." He went toward the bedroom.

"White," Nicholas called after him, "if you've got it."

Lissa handed him a glass. The woman returned with an assortment of jars on a plastic tray. Oregano, sage, tarragon—they were all whites or blacks.

"I hope you know what you're doing," Lissa said.

Nicholas shook his head as the guy brought out a white shirt with black buttons. "I'm making something," he said. "Step back. And get me a lighter."

"No lighter," the guy said.

"Matches?" the woman asked.

"That'll work."

She hesitated. She asked, "Will all this fix your eyes?"

Nicholas paused. He didn't know exactly what he was doing. He drew from a variety of the arts he had practiced and played with, but mostly the best he could do—even here so far—was a little bit of light. Okay, here there had been a substantial amount of light, beyond anything he'd ever conjured before. But he needed something big now, something unique, and since he didn't have a spell to make precisely what he needed, he was improvising. What it would accomplish, in the end, he didn't know. He didn't have a plan that stretched so far as fixing his eyes. He suspected they were their normal brown, and there had never been reds outside of the neon on this side of the mirror.

From outside, from above on the roof, one of the dogs howled. Everyone froze, if only for a moment.

The guy went to shut his window. It had already let Nicholas and Lissa in, wasn't that enough? The howl was wolf-like, and it was answered, and the answer was none too distant.

"Yes," Nicholas answered, because anything else would require the same explanations he needed. But he paused again. "Hey, what's your name?"

"Us?" the woman asked.

"Don't think anyone's ever asked us before," the guy said.

"You're kidding."

"Honestly," the woman said, "he doesn't remember much. He's Dane. I'm Devi." She gave a white jeans curtsey.

He smiled. "Thank you, Devi. Dane. This means a lot to me."

"Yeah," Dane said. "It's a crazy world out there."

"I'm Nicholas. The woman with the gun, she's Lissa."

"I'm dangerous," Lissa warned them.

Devi shook her head. "You ain't as dangerous as you think. Have you seen the sky?" Everyone glanced toward the window, the one which had been open a few minutes ago. One of the dogs stared in at them, salivating, growling from the back of its throat, black barbed wire fur matted back. It was raining. The rain was neon red, like the dog's eyes.

Devi drew the curtain over the window. "Enough of that," she said. "You've got work to do."

Nicholas filled the glass with the herbs and mixed

them with his forefinger. They didn't have to be evenly distributed, just plentiful and pungent. He dumped some of the herbs on the front of the shirt, between two mother of pearl buttons, and the rest on the other half the shirt, between button holes.

Everyone watched in silence—well, in the pounding silence of the red rain—as Nicholas struck the match and brought the flame down to the herbs on one side. They caught quickly, unnaturally, and burnt in a flash. He lit the other side off the same match. Each side left stains in the shirt, one representing this apartment, the other the abandoned Palace Theater. He drew the two sides together and fastened the two buttons, so that the two locations were adjacent.

"I see what you did," Devi said.

As another dog howled outside, Nicholas said, "Let's just hope it works."

Lissa went to the apartment door and pulled it open, revealing not the stage or auditorium of the Palace Theater, but a small apartment, with the abandoned spring frame of a twin sized bed and a table which might once have supported a lamp: the manager's apartment over the theater, all the different shades of black overlapping.

"Welcome," Nicholas said, echoing the words they'd heard earlier, "to the Palace Theater."

EIGHT

"How," Nicholas asked, "do you think we're going to get back there? You saw what happened on the roofs. You saw there's no place to go."

"Down," Lissa said.

"Underground?"

"There's more to this world than you imagine," the guy said, lounging back on the couch. "What you need, if you want it, is a map."

"Have you got one?"

"Damn straight, I do. Hey, Devi!"

A woman emerged from the bedroom. "You rang, master?" The sarcasm was vivid, but her smirk cut it back to something playful.

"No, baby, I didn't mean nothing like that," the

71

guy said. "I just need to know, have you still got those pamphlets? From the subway?"

She eyed him, then looked at Nicholas with his gun. "You ain't as dangerous as you think," she told him. "Have you seen the sky?"

They all glanced through the open window. It was dark out there, not just nighttime dark but strangely iridescent, burgundy or maroon, a color Nicholas could barely register. He went to the window and looked up, over the alley, into clouds that were bubbling, spinning and whirling, with tendrils of smoke dancing like tentacles in a New England speakeasy. And closer, on top of the roof, looking down at him, were the dogs, a dozen or more, staring, salivating.

The rain started then. A red rain. Nicholas slammed shut the window, drew a curtain, and said, "We should focus."

Devi had found the subway map. They laid it out on the floor, over the impossible color of the carpet. They unfolded it. They spent forever unfolding it. It hadn't been that thick, but there was as much paper as there was space. On one side, in the tiniest letters imaginable, were the timetables for a variety of rail lines. On the other, a map that resembled a circuit board.

"I can't do anything with this," Nicholas said.

"We're here," Devi said, pointing with a razor sharp red fingernail and poking a hole in the map.

"And you want to get here," the guy said, also

pointing. His finger was dirty and smudged and dull, and did not put a hole in the paper. Nicholas thought that was significant. He thought a lot of things were significant, including the fact that the guy had no name, and was therefore expendable. When he looked at Devi, she met his eye, and he couldn't catch the details of her through her perfection.

"Hey," Lissa said, snapping her fingers in front of his face. "Focus."

"Right." Nicholas swallowed. "I don't see the theater on this map."

"Trust me," the guy said, "that's the right place."

"Of course it is," Lissa said. "Have you never taken the subway?"

"I like to give my legs the exercise."

"You're infuriating."

"The alleys are all twisted," Nicholas said, "and the rooftops looked like they never break for streets. How do we know we can trust this map?"

"I never did," the guy said. "But it's all you've got."

"No," Lissa said. She turned to Devi. "Have you got gloves? I don't mean winter gloves, I mean..."

"I know what you mean." Devi went for the bedroom.

"You," Lissa said, putting out a palm, "I need a bullet. From that gun."

"You need a bullet?"

"Actually, I need the gunpowder." Then she turned

to the guy who had been watching TV. "I need thread. Have you got any?"

"If we don't, we can pull some off one of my old shirts. Them things are just unravelling."

"I'll make that work," Lissa said.

"What is it you think you're doing?" Nicholas asked.

"I'm not entirely sure," Lissa said, "but I think I only need one more thing." She looked at Devi again, who had returned with a pair of gloves like you might see on the fancy ladies at a 1929 opera house. "Thimble?"

Devi shook her head. "Not here."

"I...I don't want to get blood on this," Lissa said. "I'm not that good a seamstress."

Devi sat opposite Lissa. "Enough of this," she said. "You've got work to do."

Lissa spread the gunpowder over the pertinent section of the map. It seemed like a long distance. From outside, from on the fire escape, one of the dogs howled. Everyone froze, if only for a moment. The howl was wolf-like, and it was answered, and the answer came from the roof above them.

"A lighter?" Lissa asked.

Devi got a book of matches from the kitchen. Lissa struck one, then set the little flame to the gunpowder. It burned in a flash, distorting the map, obscuring the parts that weren't needed and leaving a clear path from this apartment to the Palace Theater.

Lissa produced a needle, apparently plucking it from the air unless she'd had one hidden in her jeans or hair or something. She ran the thread through the eye of the needle, then went to work on the map, stitching with crazy speed. With a tug, she pulled the two locations together on the map. With the last stitch, she drew blood, and a drop smudged the ink on the map.

"Damn." Lissa sucked at her finger. "That hurt."

"I see what you did," Devi said. "That's not a good omen."

As another dog howled outside, Nicholas said, "There are no more good omens."

"Did it work?" Nicholas asked. He got up, went to the apartment door, and pulled it open onto a room that had clearly not been there before, a room with a neatly made bed and a table with a lamp: the manager's apartment over the theater, in soft pastel colors Nicholas couldn't even register.

"Welcome," Nicholas said, echoing the words they'd heard earlier, "to the Palace Theater."

NINE

The step across the threshold made them all dizzy. They swayed and shifted, they grabbed each other for support. Nicholas held onto the wall. It was like an elevator suddenly plunging beneath him. He barely kept his footing. He stumbled into the abandoned apartment, through a whorl of dust and cobwebs. The floor creaked under his step.

Lissa patted down her dress. "That," she said, "was impressive."

"We still have to get downstairs," Nicholas said. "Through the dogs."

"And the man with the spotlight," Lissa said. "Maybe we should go after him first."

Nicholas shook his head. "I doubt he's still there, but

since I don't know the way—let's see what we see first."

"Man, that was something special," Dale said.

"We're just getting started," Lissa said. She went to pull the door open and had to really work at it. Time had warped the wood of the door, had settled it into place, and it was not happy to move. Devi came alongside her to help. When the door gave way, it gave all the way, and swung open wildly.

On the other side: a dark hallway. Nicolas pushed the ball of light ahead of them to light their way. It might draw attention, but it would also prevent surprises. Under his breath, he said a few words he didn't even know, ancient words of protection borrowed from shriveled memories. He must've read a passage in a book at some point.

As yet, they had no idea which way the stage was. The hall might be on a side, directly above, or all the way at the back of the auditorium. Nicholas chose a direction at random. There was no subtly in walking on these floors, as they creaked, cracked, and squealed with every step. The dogs had made no noise. Nicholas considered casting something for stealth, but he didn't know how much he could do before depleting himself. Any little thing might be one thing too many if it came to a confrontation.

At the end of the hall, stairs led down and a door led to the right.

"Could be the lighting," Lissa whispered. She pointed the gun as Devi opened the door.

It was, in fact, the spotlight, still aimed directly at the stage. The mirror stood there, grungy and facing away, unguarded.

"He had been here," Lissa said.

Nicholas nodded. "Now, he's probably at Dale's place." He looked over his shoulder. "Did we shut the door behind us?"

Nothing moved in the hallway, nothing emerged from the manager's apartment, nothing made a sound that could be heard over the drumbeats of the red rain.

"We've got to assume they're coming," Lissa said.

"All we have to do," Nicholas said, "is reach the mirror on that stage."

"What's so special about the mirror?" Dale asked.

Devi smacked his shoulder. "Isn't it obvious?"

Nicholas took a breath and started down the stairs. These had never been meant for the masses. They were the opposite of grand and opulent, and each step seemed to sag beneath his weight. He didn't want to touch the walls, and his ball of light, bobbing along beside him, revealed nothing comforting. They descended to a storeroom. The skeletons of big old desks leaned against the walls. A few crates had been left behind. Mice, maybe rats, scurried out of the reach of the light.

The storeroom led to an office. On top of the desk, on a sheet of fresh paper, someone had hastily drawn circles and triangles. The cracked remnants of pencil leads littered the desk.

"Someone's been here," Dale said, peering at the desk.

"A ghost?" Devi suggested.

"Something else," Nicholas said, as additional shapes formed. They were rough, they were incomplete, they were crazed, and they were leaking to this side of the mirror from someplace else, someplace where the Palace Theater still entertained guests. "It's a good sign, I think."

"An omen?" Lissa asked.

Nicholas didn't answer. He didn't know how. But the pencils that were making those circles, and the circles themselves, were not the same charcoal black as everything else in this world.

Through the office, they reached the lobby. Nicholas wanted to run. He wanted to race. He said, "I'll have to face the mirror alone."

"No," Lissa said, grabbing his hand long enough to give a reassuring squeeze.

The lobby seemed to be a geometric impossibility, folding in and around itself, curved in ways Nicholas didn't understand. It wasn't an exact duplicate of the Palace Theater lobby he had known. It was something else entirely, something strange, something unsettling.

"The illusionist," voices said, voices that didn't really reach across from the other side of the mirror. "The artist." "The virtuoso himself." It sounded vaguely hostile. "Do a trick. Give us a preview."

"Am I the only one hearing that?" Nicholas asked.

Dale said, "I don't hear nothing."

"Do us a magic!"

Dale jumped, startled.

"We all heard that," Devi said.

"Ghosts?" Dale asked.

Nicholas shook his head. Lissa said, "We must be getting closer."

"This way," someone said, someone solid, someone on this side of the mirror. An usher stood at an open side door. "What do you think you're doing out there? Someone will see you."

Nicholas blinked. "Who?"

The usher waved them into the room. "They'll simply eat you alive if they find you."

"That can't be a good thing," Nicholas admitted.

The usher showed his teeth in what was meant as a grin. "Of course not."

"You realize," Lissa said, as they stepped into the side room, "you're an usher in an abandoned theater."

"The Parliament of Ushers," he said, "would never allow a theater to be forsaken."

"Do you know what's going on?" Nicholas asked.

The usher shook his head. "I had hoped you might. I'm here only to protect the theater, and I will do what I can to stop this. At first, I thought you were responsible."

"Me?"

"Wielding all that magic," the usher said, shaking his head. "A natural assumption."

"We need to get Nicholas to the stage," Lissa said.

The usher shook his head. "Right now, no place in the Palace Theater is safe, especially not the stage."

"And this room?" Devi asked.

The usher shrugged. "Not exactly a place in the theater."

"The stage," Lissa said again.

"You'll have to go through the Throne of..." The usher checked himself. "You'll have to go through the auditorium. I should warn you, there are stairs on both sides of the stage, but this was never a playhouse. So, while there's no real altar for the orchestra, there's still a pit in front for the organist."

"Right," Nicholas said. "The sides."

"You may have to fight your way through," the usher told him.

"And who are you, exactly?" Dale asked. "I mean, it seems like you're trying to help and all, and man I can dig that, I can, but I ain't never heard of no Parliament of Ushers."

"Call me Algernon," the usher said. "I've got sigils in place to contain the theater's ghosts, but anything from the outside, I cannot control." He looked at each of them in turn, deciding something, and finally nodded. "Good luck, and good hunting." He leaned closer to Nicholas and added in a whisper: "I would have constrained the lot of you if I thought it would resolve things."

NINE

Crossing the threshold delivered a wave of dizziness. Nicholas grabbed the wall for support. Lissa held onto him. It was like a roller coaster hitting its first decline at ninety miles an hour. He stumbled into the apartment, into another vast explosion of color. But it wasn't as harsh as it had been, and he managed to keep his feet and not get sick. "That," he said, "was impressive."

"We still have to get downstairs," Lissa said. "Through the dogs."

He smiled for her, and for Devi. The guy from the apartment led the way into the hall. The hall was dark, but there was a light at one end of it, so when they started in that direction Nicholas didn't complain. He wasn't as interested in the mirror as he was the man who had sicked the dogs after them.

They moved silently across the carpeted hall until they reached stairs and a door. Without discussion or delay, Nicholas pulled open the door and went through, onto a small landing where the spotlight was still warm. The rest of the auditorium was dark, but the mirror remained on stage, angled just so that he couldn't see it.

A mirror—not that one—had been the source of all this, hadn't it? Nicholas didn't want to consider it too closely.

Lissa pulled shut the door. "What if the dogs were there?" she asked in a furious whisper. "What if their master was there?"

"I was kinda hoping he would be," Nicholas said.

"If he was following you," Devi said, "then he's probably in our apartment now."

Lissa looked back. "Did we shut the door behind us?"

The hall remained empty. Quiet. Unmoving. Nicholas tightened his fists in anticipation and lowered his eyes. Half a minute passed. An entire minute. He was beginning to feel foolish.

"If the magic is sympathetic to us," Lissa said, "then perhaps they can't get through."

"Or they're not in our apartment yet," the guy said.

"We've got to assume they're coming," Lissa said. "Behind and ahead. All we have to do is reach that mirror."

"What's so special about the mirror?" the guy asked.

Devi smacked his shoulder. "Isn't it obvious?"

Through this, Nicholas tried to listen, maybe to something inside the theater but maybe something inside himself. He considered options. He considered the weight of the 9mm. It felt lighter, now, by one bullet. With the red rain pounding on the roof, all other sounds were hollow. Nicholas said, "Downstairs. To the stage."

Nicholas went first to the stairs. These were not meant for the public; those stairs would be grand and sweep them onto the balcony. These were stairs for the workers, straight and unadorned and direct. They didn't lead to the lobby where people would gather before the event and buy fancy wine, but to a storeroom. Boxes. Desks. Ledgers. Maybe money, too, but Nicholas wasn't alone and didn't appreciate an audience. He only had to look at her to remember this wasn't his Lissa.

The storeroom led to an office, where a man hunched over the desk scribbling furiously on paper. He looked up, just for the moment, and said, "Come to pay your respects, have you?" The voice was enough to tell Nicholas this wasn't the man who had aimed the spotlight earlier. A glance at the papers showed he was making circles and triangles and breaking the lead on a lot of pencils.

Through the office, Nicholas reached the lobby, Lissa

and Devi and the guy from the apartment immediately behind him. He wanted to run. He wanted to race. He needed to face the mirror alone.

But the lobby wasn't empty.

Nicholas tried to back up, but there were too many people behind him. And too many in front of him. The lobby was filled with them. Men, women, children, all suddenly making noise, talking, laughing, drinking champagne. Some were in tuxedos and fancy dresses, others torn jeans and tee shirts, and all levels between. The lobby seemed to fold in over itself so it could fit more people.

Then someone pointed and said, "There he is!"

A thousand pairs of eyes turned toward Nicholas. "The illusionist!" someone cried. "The artist!" "The virtuoso himself!" That was followed by, "Do a trick! Give us a preview!"

Nicholas glanced at Lissa. She winked. "You were never the talent," she told him.

"Do us a magic!"

Lissa snapped a finger and the lights flashed off. When they came back on, streamers were falling from the ceiling. The crowd cheered and raised their hands and danced.

"This way," one of the ushers said quickly, guiding them away from the stairs and away from the auditorium to another office. The usher wiped his brow and demanded, "What do you think you're doing? These people haven't bought any tickets!"

Nicholas blinked. "What?"

"No tickets," the usher said, "no show. That's how it works."

"We don't need any tickets," Devi said.

"Of course not, I know that," the usher said. "You're with the performers. I get that. I do. But all those people out there—they'll simply eat you alive if they can."

"That can't be a good thing," Nicholas admitted.

The usher showed his teeth in what was meant as a grin. "Of course not."

"And who are you, exactly?" Nicholas asked.

"Call me Ignatius," the usher said. "I'm here only to protect the theater. I thought you might be responsible, but..." He hesitated. "You don't seem to be."

"Do you know what's going on?" Devi asked.

"We need to get to the stage," Lissa said.

"You can't go around through the back," Ignatius said. "You'll have to go through the Throne...the auditorium. There are stairs on either side, but I can't vouch for their safety. And though there's no real altar for the orchestra, there is still a pit in front, and the Wurlitzer."

"An organ," Devi said, "might return some powerful magic of its own, wouldn't it?"

Ignatius narrowed his eyes at her, then turned to

Lissa. "You may have to fight your way through."

"I've got a little bit of magic of my own, apparently," Lissa said.

The usher shook his head. "I've constrained the ghosts of the theater, but as yet, I can do nothing about outside influences. There are...a great many of them. The people in that lobby, they are real, as best I can tell, actual people, not ghosts and not from elsewhere, but they are not in their own minds."

"We'll be careful."

"Be more than careful," Ignatius told her. "Be swift."

"Man, can I run when I have to," the guy from the apartment said.

Devi swatted his arm. "Shush."

Nicholas withdrew his gun and said to Ignatius, "We'll be doubly careful."

Ignatius looked at the gun for a long moment, then met Nicholas' eyes. He considered something, decided something, finally even nodded to himself. "I would have retrained the lot of you, if I thought it would resolve things. Don't make me reconsider."

Nicholas grinned. "You don't have to worry about us."

As Ignatius stepped back, he raised his hands as if to say he had no part in this. He said, "Good luck."

TEN

The four of them waded back into the lobby. The crowd pressed close, jostling, spilling their drinks, apologizing, recognizing the magician out of uniform. Music piped in through tinny speakers scattered in the ceiling. They called for tricks, they called for magic, they called for tickets so they could see the show. They pushed and pulled and made a roadblock, driving them away from the auditorium doors.

"Do something," Nicholas told Lissa, "or I will."

She nodded. She split away, headed toward the center. Devi and her man flanked Nicholas, but the tide was impenetrable and constantly in motion.

With some distance between them, Lissa lifted her hands and announced, "Butterflies!" Her voice broke through the noise of the crowd and brought an instance of silence, a brief and beautiful lull in the cacophony. Many, maybe most—but not quite all—eyes turned to Lissa. She started flicking her wrists, tossing quick butterflies out of her hands. They were slashes of neon green and pink. They crackled with electricity. They fluttered for just a few seconds before dissipating.

But it was enough. Faces turned at the spectacle. Lissa threw the butterflies up and in every direction. She threw them one at a time, then in pairs, then in triplets, and the ozone smell of them filled the lobby. That wasn't a natural neon smell, but a result of Lissa's magic.

Nicholas used the distraction to push forward. At the double doors to the auditorium, The usher—not Ignatius—gave Nicholas a brief nod and pushed the door open only enough for a person to get through. Devi and her man followed him into the brightened auditorium.

A sea of burgundy seats greeted them, thick burgundy drapes, brilliant gold accents and architectural flourishes—the combination of which momentarily blinded Nicholas. This wasn't his side of the mirror, and the sudden explosions of colors, even these rich, dark colors, impacted him. Devi and her man caught him from either side. Supported him. The guy said, "We're almost to the stage."

This wasn't Nicholas's idea, but he didn't know what

else to do. He staggered forward, and that's when he heard the dogs. The growling and snarling. They were in the seats, and in the aisles, and everywhere Nicholas could see.

He drew the gun and shot the dog directly ahead of him. Like thunder, the shot cracked the night, and cracked the sounds of the theater. Behind them, the lobby went silent. Lissa burst into the auditorium from the other set of doors. An usher pulled the doors shut against the swelling audience.

"Run!" Lissa yelled, and she tossed a bolt of her own, lightning, a jagged arc of it that split and struck three of the dogs. They yelped. Nicholas stepped over the fallen dog ahead of him, the guy beside him. Devi, however, remained at the back of the aisle. They drove forward, through the screaming animals, creatures so unlike dogs he no longer understood the comparison. They snapped at him. The guy caught one as it leapt through the air, caught it with his forearms, struggled to keep its jaws from clamping shut. Nicholas shot another. Lissa conjured another volley of lightning. It came so close, it scorched Nicholas's nose.

The steps alongside the stage were blocked, so he went up the middle. He almost leapt into the pit, but it was deeper than he'd expected. He'd never get up before those dogs tore him apart. So he leapt onto the organ stand instead, crashing onto the keys of the organ, sending a tumultuous sounds resounding through the pipes on either side of the stage. He clamored over the Wurlitzer organ, shooting one more dog directly in his path, and leapt onto the stage.

Nicholas lost his balance.

He tipped backwards, but the guy from the apartment was there, right behind him, and stopped Nicholas from falling. Then the dogs got to Devi's man, one on his leg, another on his arm, and a third going for the throat.

The man without a name stumbled backwards, off the organ stand, into the pit where a dozen dogs fell instantly upon him. Another jolt of lightning, a cry from the back of the theater, even three more gunshots from the gun in Nicholas's hand, were not enough to save his life.

The rest of the dogs, smelling blood, moved more swiftly.

Nicholas reached the mirror. Turned it on the stage so he could look directly into it. Lissa reached him then, so the two of them stared into the mirror at images of themselves staring back, which, honestly, should have been what they expected.

"Do something," Lissa said from the inside the mirror.

And her Nicholas, the one on the other side of the mirror, reached forward. Nicholas reached, too, and when they both touched the surface of the mirror, Nicholas didn't feel the cool smooth surface but his own hand, warm flesh, grasping him. The Nicholas in the mirror pulled. Nicholas pulled back. Lissa pulled with them on both sides.

Lissa muttered something magical.

The other Lissa said, "We're ruined here. Pull us through."

And that's what they did.

The mirror shattered as the reflections of Nicholas and Lissa joined Nicholas and Lissa on the stage. The dogs suddenly scattered. The lights dimmed noticeably. Nicholas, having used up as much of himself as he could, slumped, and only Lissa's support kept him from crumbling to the floor.

Lissa and her reflection went to Devi, who seemed ready to drop into the pit after her man. The dogs were gone, but they'd left only a mess.

"I didn't even know his name," Nicholas whispered.

"Dale," his reflection told him. "His name was Dale, and he died protecting us."

Devi, makeup streaked down her face, looked up at the two versions of Nicholas. "He was mine," she said. "Mine, and mine alone. You—your enemy—had no right to take him from me." With that final word, the theater rumbled.

"I'm not sure what we accomplished," Lissa said to Nicholas. "Whatever's wrong with the world, it's still wrong. And now..."

"Now," Lissa's reflection said, "there's two of us."

"And what happened on our side of the mirror," Nicholas's reflection said, "was terrible. We lost everything. All of it. The whole world collapsed, and only we escaped it."

Nicholas stared at his reflection. He wasn't full color like the rest of this world, but of a similar palette, if darker and in higher contrast. He said, to everyone, "This may be bigger than we thought."

TEN

The four of them returned to the lobby. Nicholas could smell the ozone of the ghosts in the darkness. This theater had once been vibrant. Exciting. Now, memories and inertia were all the held it together.

Nicholas heard the crowds from across the mirror. He didn't know how he knew the source, but he knew. They called for tricks, they called for magic, they called for tickets so they could see the show, but they did so elsewhere. Nicholas's fists crackled with electricity. Little pastel butterflies leaked from his hands, tiny things that fluttered once and ceased to exist.

Devi put a hand on his shoulder when he paused to look at these. "Energy leaks," she said, her voice suggesting this was some sort of reassurance.

At the double doors, Nicholas pushed, and put some muscle into it, to force the door open enough for a single person to slip through. He went first, and sent a ball of light ahead to the center of the auditorium. It rose above the seats, all ragged black, like the shreds that remained of drapes. The architectural flourishes and accents were all in white, the color palette familiar now and expected but no less stark.

They were not alone in the theater. There were the dog things. A hundred dogs or a thousand in the seats, in the aisles, at the top of the stairs leading to the stage, all growling and salivating.

Lissa lifted her gun and shot the first dog.

That set them all into motion.

Nicholas twisted his fingers and launched spectral variations of himself down the other aisle, fooling ome of the dogs went that way. He launched arcs of electricity from his miniature sun at the center of the theater. The beasts, which could hardly be called dogs, howled and yelped and avoided the blasts, but still came for them.

"We're almost to the stage," Dale said, pushing forward.

The dogs snapped their toothed jaws and lunged and seemed intent on protecting the stage. This, as much as anything else, propelled Nicholas. It confirmed they were moving in the right direction.

So Nicholas drove forward. Lissa shouted curses as

she spent bullets on the endless dogs. Nicholas launched two more balls of light into the theater, from which bolts of lightning helped clear their path, but the effort nearly made him lose his balance. Devi and Dale caught him, from either side, and helped him keep his feet.

Then Dale caught one of the dogs in his hands. Caught it at the jaws. Before it could tear him apart, Lissa shot the dog, but her next pull of the trigger rang hollow.

At the stairs, all of six steps, they kicked at the dogs. Lissa smashed one with the butt of the gun. Nicholas muzzled one with a pastel construct that would linger no longer than the butterflies. Dale, trying to catch another, toppled over, fell to his knees at the very front of the stage, and tumbled into the narrow organ pit and more of the dogs, like alligators, waiting with open jaws. They fell on him. A blast of electricity from Nicholas's hands—which burned his fingers—and a hellish cry from Devi, were insufficient to save him.

The rest of the dogs, smelling blood, moved more swiftly.

Nicholas reached the mirror. He shifted it so he could look directly in. With Devi at the edge of the stage watching the dogs rend Dale in a frenzy, the mirror reflected only Nicholas and Lissa. The two of them stared at themselves. What else had they expected?

"Do something," Lissa said from the other side of the mirror.

Her Nicholas, the one on the other side of the mirror,

reached forward. Nicholas reached, too, and when they touched the surface of the mirror, Nicholas didn't feel the cool smooth surface but his own hand, warm flesh, grasping his. The Nicholas in the mirror pulled. Nicholas pulled back. Lissa pulled with them on both sides.

Nicholas muttered something magical.

The other Nicholas said, "It's ruined here. Pull us through."

And that's what they did.

The mirror shattered as the reflections of Nicholas and Lissa joined Nicholas and Lissa on the stage. The dogs suddenly scattered.

Lissa and her reflection went to Devi, who had reached the stage and seemed ready to drop into the pit after Dale. The dogs were gone, but they'd left a mess of the man.

"I didn't even know his name," Nicholas's reflection said.

"Dale," Nichols told him. "His name was Dale, and he died protecting us."

Devi, makeup streaked down her face, looked up at the two versions of Nicholas. "He was mine," she said. "Mine, and mine alone. You—your enemy—had no right to take him from me." With that final word, the theater rumbled.

"I'm not sure what we accomplished," Nicholas admitted, kneeling beside Devi and putting an arm around her. "I'm so, so sorry. I wish I could have done something to prevent this."

"We couldn't prevent any of it," Nicholas's reflection said. "On our side of the mirror, the whole world fragmented into dust. We were barely able to get out, and in the end, we only escaped because of you."

Nicholas and his reflection stared at each other a moment longer. The reflection was not black and white like this world. He was almost darker than Nicholas, but of a similar color palette. Nicholas said, "This may be bigger than we thought."

ELEVEN

Devi and the two Lissas looked at Nicholas and his reflection.

"Isn't it obvious?" Nicholas's reflection asked.

"This reflection didn't come from your side of the mirror," Nicholas told Lissa.

"And this reflection didn't come from your side," Nicholas's reflection told Lissa's reflection.

"Here," Nicholas said, "the colors—if you can call them that—are all black and white, but scratchy, dry, brittle looking."

"Looks normal to me," Lissa said.

"Because it is normal for you," Nicholas said.

"But not," Nicholas's reflection added, "for me. Our colors are sharper, richer, more thorough."

"Then this," Lissa said, "was the wrong mirror."

100

Nicholas shook his head. "How can there be a wrong mirror? Wouldn't all mirrors reflect the same thing?"

"Of course not," Devi said. She wiped tears from her face with the back of a hand. "In the long history of glass, there have been innumerable variations in the strength of mirrors, the chemical composition, the amount of mercury or aluminum, even the thickness of the glass. Even from a machine, even when they are mass produced, every mirror is its own thing. And every mirror has something like what you would call a soul."

Everyone stared at Devi. She rose as she spoke. "In times past, men sought to travel the paths between mirrors, but they were fools, or foolish, and they failed to understand a basic fact about mirrors, the same basic fact you've failed to understand today. Each mirror is unique."

"But," Nicholas said, "the mirror where this all started—it's been shattered."

"On my side, too," Nicholas's reflection said.

"Can we repair it somehow?" Lissa asked.

"With what?" Devi asked. "Glue? Adhesive? That would change the mirror's nature, and therefore its reflection."

"I have a question," Lissa's reflection said. "If there's more than one of each of us, on every side of every mirror, how do we know your mirror is the one that started it all?"

"I would think it was mine," Nicholas's reflection said, glancing at the fragments of mirror on the stage floor. "But there's nothing there."

"That," Lissa's reflection told him, "was my world that was destroyed, not yours."

"It's a good question," Lissa said, "but it's philosophical, and we need to do something practical."

"Go back to my shattered mirror?" Nicholas asked.

"Not your mirror," Lissa told him, "but your reflection's mirror." She glanced at his reflection and added, "Not yours. The reflection he switched with. Yours is on the other side of that."

Nicholas took a breath. He was weak, but not defeated. "What's it like outside?"

"Doesn't matter," Nicholas's reflection said. "We still have the map." The balled-up shirt was in his hand.

Nicholas accepted the shirt. It was very similar to Dale's shirt he had worked on. The map had been made in the same way, with the same ingredients, and it felt warm in his hand. He reflection smiled at him. No, he grinned.

The map included Dale's apartment. The map included the theater. And the map included Nicholas's apartment. His hadn't.

"It needs," Nicholas's reflection said, "a bit of magic."

Nicholas laid it out on the floor, over the dark, dead mirror shards. He spread it out, examined it, and realized what was wrong. "It's backwards," Nicholas said, "and backwards again." He shook his head. "I can barely read it."

"Make it yours," Nicholas's reflection said.

Nicholas considered this. This map might be relevant, but not here. They could go back and get the one he'd made, but it didn't include his apartment. He hadn't thought that far ahead.

He picked up one of the shards and, quickly, pricked his finger. A thick drop of blood rolled free. He squeezed it over cloth map until it fell. The blood splattered their current location, the Palace Theater, and briefly the whole theater flashed neon red. Something rumbled outside, a low, long, deep threat of thunder.

He rubbed the blood into the shirt with his wound, saturating it, spreading it as far as it would go, from apartment to apartment, then undid the button. As he did this, Lissa and her reflection cleared the jams in their 9mms—apparently, they each had one last bullet. He pulled the edge of the shirt down, and realigned the holes so that the apartment next to the theater, on the other side of the shirt, would no longer be Dale's but his. His reflection's. He took a deep breath, closed the button, and said, "That should be it."

Algernon watched from the rear of the theater as they left through the stage door.

On the other side: Nicholas's apartment, utterly familiar and completely unknown. The walls were where his walls had always been. The old apartment was like his, but without the color. The walls were black like charcoal and white like chalk. Everything in the room, the desk and tables, the chairs, the lamps, all sketched in variations of these. The bulb glowing on the lamp gave off a bright, distinct white light, more substantive than should be, thicker, cleaner.

"This looks vaguely familiar," Nicholas's reflection said.

There were books, and a deck of cards which Nicholas pocketed as he and his reflection walked through the apartment.

"It's not exactly mine," Nicholas's reflection said, nudging a basket full of credit cards and cash.

"Nor mine," Nicholas said. They came around to the side of the table, to the notebooks and pens, the compass, the burnt out candle, the standing wall mirror and the sea of broken glass beneath it. Nicholas and his reflection knelt simultaneously and stared into the pieces. A dozen other reflections stared back.

"What were you trying to accomplish?" Lissa asked.

"I wanted to walk through the realms of mists," Nicholas's reflection said.

"I was trying to perfect a piece of true magic," Nicholas said.

"What kind of magic?" Lissa asked.

"Transportational," Nicholas said. "Step from one side of the theater to the other without...well, without the traditional use of mirrors."

"That," Lissa's reflection said, "sounds dubious."

"It was," Nicholas said. "Obviously. It let us here. All of us." There were four of them now. Devi had remained in the theater.

Nicholas looked down at his reflections again. Some reached for him. Some were turning away. Some were screaming, pounding against the glass. Some were simply staring. "I did this."

"No," another Nicholas said, emerging from the bedroom with two of those dogs straining at their leashes. "I did this."

ELEVEN

Devi and the two Lissa's looked at Nicholas and his reflection.

"It's obvious," Lissa said, looking directly at Nicholas's reflection. "You're not the Nicholas I knew. Neither of you is."

"How many sides of the mirror are there?" Nicholas asked.

"How many sides are there of a snowflake?" Devi asked, looking up at them and wiping tears from her face with the back of her hand. "The quantity and purity of the quicksilver, its intensity, its elasticity and its volatility. Alchemists have tried to tame it, scientists have tried to define it, madmen have ingested it in search of magical curatives or visions. And glassworkers have harnessed its reflective properties to build better mirrors. But the lead also contributes to the makeup of a mirror, and the glass contributes to its traits, and every mirror, even when they are mass produced, is its own thing. Every mirror has something like what you would call a soul."

Everyone stared at Devi. She rose as she spoke. "You, Nicholas, on this side of the mirror and the other, were a fool to try to tap into something beyond comprehension. You failed to understand the same basic fact every other practitioner and maven and adventurer has failed to understand. Each mirror is unique."

"My mirror was shattered," Nicholas said. "The mirror where all this started."

"Mine is lost," Nicholas's reflection said, looking down at the shards scattered across the stage.

"Well, we can't simply glue it back together," Lissa said. Then she looked at Devi. "Can we?"

Devi shook her head.

Lissa's reflection held up a piece of the broken mirror. "This is inert, now," she said. "Dark, non-reflective. Dead. The world on the other side of that mirror, my world, the place where I was born and lived and studied and strove, is gone." She put a hand on the shoulder of Nicholas's reflection. "Yours, too. That's why we tried to come here. We wanted to...help."

"Help how?" Nicholas asked.

"Uniting," Nicholas's reflection said. "And to do that, we need to get back to your shattered mirror. Or through that mirror, to the other side, where it all began."

Nicholas glanced at Lissa. His Lissa? He didn't completely understand, but Lissa was nodding as if this all made perfect sense.

"We still," Lissa's reflection said, producing the subway pamphlet, "have a map." She laid it out on the floor. The two Lissa's knelt next to it. Nicholas and his reflection leaned over to watch.

"It's a reflection of a reflection," Lissa said, shaking her head.

"Make it yours," her reflection told her.

"I can barely read it."

"It needs," her reflection said, "a bit of magic."

Nicholas pointed. "That's my apartment, or my reflection's apartment. My other reflection."

Lissa's reflection handed her a needle.

Lissa nodded, then pricked her finger. A drop of blood swelled there. She squeezed it over the paper map until the drop fell. The blood splattered on their current location, the Palace Theater, and briefly the whole theater flashed red. Something rumbled outside, a low, long, deep threat of thunder.

Then she unraveled the previous thread and re-used it, connecting the theater with Nicholas's apartment.

As he watched, he and his reflection glanced at each other. They shared a grin. They shared a wink. They were of one mind.

Ignatius watched from the back of the theater as they left through the stage door.

On the other side: Nicholas's apartment, utterly familiar and completely unknown. The walls were where his walls had always been. The old apartment was his, but the colors were changed. In its place, the walls were sick with color, lurid, nearly overwhelming. The bulb glowing on the lamp gave off a pale, dirty variation of light.

"This looks vaguely familiar," Nicholas's reflection said.

There were books, cards, coins, rope, boxes, and wands. Inwardly, Nicholas sneered at the collection. Had he, on this side of the mirror, no spirit of adventure, no taste for romance? "It's not exactly mine," he said.

"Nor mine," his reflection said. They came around to the side of the table, to the notebooks and pens, the compass, the burnt out candle, the standing wall mirror and the sea of broken glass beneath it. Nicholas and his reflection knelt simultaneously and stared into the pieces. A dozen other reflections stared back.

"What were you trying to accomplish?" Lissa asked.

"I needed a way of entering places unseen," Nicholas said.

"I was attempting to look in on my rival," Nicholas's reflection said.

"Who's your rival?" Lissa asked.

Nicholas and Nicholas's reflection exchanged a

look. Then his reflection turned to Lissa, and to Lissa's reflection—Devi had remained in the theater—and said, "You."

The Lissas did something, some sort of magic thing, a conjuration of words and fingers in unison, before Nicholas or his reaction could raise their guns. They each fired one bullet, one they had reserved for such an event, one they had slipped into a pocket when giving Lissa gunpowder for her magical maps. They fired across each other, Nicholas at Lissa's reflection, Nicholas's reflection at Lissa. Their magic echoed through the room, through the whole world, possibly into all the sides of all the mirrors, but it couldn't stop lead traveling at high velocity.

They died immediately, the effects of their magic unraveling already, but it was too late. The remains of the mirror crackled and sparkled. Some of the shards went dead and dark. Some strained at the edges. Some of those multiple reflections were pulled somewhere else. Nicholas and his reflection tried to resist, but they had no magic at their command, no means of escape, and they were sucked into the vortex

TWELVE

"I did this."

"I did this."

"I did this."

Reflection after reflection emerged from the mirror. Some were bloodied and beaten. Some were armed, some with the same 9mm Oliveri Lissa and her reflection carried. Some were full color, or more than full color, while others closely matched this side of the mirror. Some were red-faced, others sickly green, others bathed in shadows. They came alone, they came in pairs, they came in groups, and they dissolved into each other almost as quickly as they arrived. There were a dozen one moment, then a hundred, then a dozen, then fifty, then half that. They arrived in a flurry, and as each arrived, or each set, the fragment of mirror they came through burst, creating more, smaller fragments. Most wore variations of what Nicholas wore. At least one wore Dale's shirt with its map on it and the buttons all done wrong. All of them, or most of them, said some variation of, "I did this," and some used other languages or voices that weren't similar to Nicholas's voice at all. It overwhelmed him, and reverberated more deeply than his bones.

Nicholas's reflection—the one who been drawn from the mirror in the theater—and Lissa and her reflection stood beside Nicholas, holding onto him, preventing him from being sucked into the tide. As Nicholas wavered, the one with the dogs laughed, and the dogs bristled, and his eyes glowed bright, bright red. He was the intruder.

"I did this," he said again, as the other reflections rose—from the mirrors—and fell—into each other and, ultimately, into the intruder. "I will no longer be your puppet, I will no longer flounder in your wake. I am no mere echo, Nicholas, but I am the truest reflection of you."

Nicholas resisted the gravity of the other reflections, the pull and the push of them all, the thunder from outside and the crackling electricity inside. He held his ground, with help.

"So many variations of you," the intruder said.

"These echoes all captured a part of you, Nicholas, and the sum total of your reflections is as great as the original. I have been working a long time, in plain sight, to achieve this."

"What, exactly, do you think you're achieving?" Lissa asked, because Nicholas could not.

"I," the intruder said, "shall replace you, and shall cease to be merely your echo."

The individual reflections, and sometimes the reflections of them, the copies of copies, some insubstantial as wind, some as powerful, continued to pour forth. The Nicholas who murdered. The Nicholas who trained boxers. The Nicholas who painted. The dancer. The sculptor. The assassin.

The thief grinned at Nicholas, and winked at the Lissa who belonged here, on this side of the mirror. His coloring matched. Nicholas reached out, grabbed him by the wrist, said, "You wouldn't betray me."

The thief laughed. "I already have." Then he stepped into the intruder, another variation folded into the whole, so that he became more and more substantial.

"My pets," the intruder said, "were made with your hair, which I collected from the shower while you slept." He released the leash. The two dogs leapt forward, snarling, gnashing teeth. Outside, thunder boomed and lightning flashed unceasingly.

Nicholas did not back down. He caught the dogs

by the throat as they leapt, one in each hand, assisted perhaps by the magic he'd been able to tap on this side of the mirror.

"You cannot resist me anymore," the intruder said. "I'm taking over."

Lissa and her reflection stepped forward, guns raised, and shot the dog-like things in the heads. The intruder laughed and stepped forward.

"There was too much of me in you," the intruder said, "to ever survive."

They were face to face now, Nicholas and the intruder. Only the one other reflection remained, who had stood beside him in the Palace Theater. The intruder reached toward the reflection.

"No," Nicholas's reflection said. "All of the reflections combined may be enough to overpower the original, but you do not have all of them." He stepped into Nicholas, directly into him. The shiver started in Nicholas's skin and resounded in his marrow.

"You're still weakened," the intruder said, grinning.

"And you," Nicholas said, "are just a pale imitation." Nicholas stepped into the intruder—not to join, not to unify, not even to overtake. He stepped in to overwhelm. He focused the magic he had mustered, the storm around them, the residual energies of the Palace Theater. He called upon the memories of loves and losses, of power surrendered and acquired and wasted.

He drew from the magicians of the past, the jugglers and escape artists, the prognosticators, the clairvoyants and telekinetics, the cardsharps and hustlers and pickpockets and conmen, the illusionists and wizards and sleight of hand artists. He used his dreams and his hopes and his fears, and he subjugated this mere echo of him until the intruder stopped laughing, until the intruder cracked and splintered and fractured, until the intruder erupted into one and a thousand pieces. They scattered around the room, this chalk and charcoal variation on his apartment, and fluttered to the ground like leaflets from the sky.

One by one, the shards of the intruder dimmed. Briefly, they retained an image of a fragment of Nicholas. They died like the pieces of mirror on the stage, gray and lifeless. The pieces dissolved into dust. The dust scattered into nothingness.

The only piece that remained looked in on Nicholas's apartment, his actual apartment. Exhausted, Nicholas fell to his knees next to it, even as Lissa and her reflection went to the window.

"There's no world out there," Lissa said. "It's collapsing."

"Like mine," Lissa's reflection said.

Nicholas nodded. "One world," he said, "remains."

The three of them passed through the fragment in the moment before everything imploded and the world, on that side of the mirror, ceased to exist.

THIRTEEN

When Nicholas finally woke, days later, he ached all over. No mirrors remained in his apartment, so he couldn't look at himself to see what had happened. The toll, however, had been tremendous.

His apartment had not suffered on his own side of the mirror as it had on the other side. There wasn't much to clean up, or it had already been cleaned. He didn't know. He found fresh milk in the fridge and swallowed two full glasses of it before venturing near the window. Outside, he saw the street he had always seen, and not a cloud in the twilight sky.

He showered. He let the hot water wash away everything, almost everything, everything he imagined he should lose. He didn't know if it was effective, but

116

he felt more awake, more alert, and more alive after he dressed and left his apartment. Down the stairs, several blocks, straight to Lissa's apartment.

She had been here. Lissa and her reflection. In fairness, they were both reflections. He wondered about the original. They had come and taken everything worth taking, clothes and jewelry and money, and had left a note on the kitchen table. It said, simply, Goodbye.

Nicholas went to the Palace Theater. Over his marquee, over the image of himself as magician, someone had plastered a sign: Cancelled. It was no great loss, but Nicholas stared at it a while anyway. He went to the door, tried it, but found it locked. Before he turned away, however, it opened from the inside. Two men stood there. Ushers. One was Algernon.

"It's over," he told them.

"It is," Algernon said gravely. "Your things have been packed and already delivered. You were responsible."

Nicholas nodded. The ushers pulled the door shut and locked it, audibly, from inside.

Nicholas turned to walk away. Not toward his apartment. He wasn't sure what he would do there anymore. In his jacket, he still had a deck of cards from the other side of the mirror, a deck colored in streaks of charcoal and chalk. He manipulated the cards as he walked away from everything.

Eventually, he realized he wasn't alone.

"What now?" Devi asked him.

"I don't know."

Eventually, Devi said, "I forgive you. Dale—you weren't responsible for him. You weren't responsible for any of it, no matter what the ushers think."

"And Lissa."

Devi smiled. "She doesn't blame you, either, I'm sure. She had her own thing going on. Maybe you didn't notice."

"I don't know if I did," Nicholas said. "Will I see her—them—again?"

"Maybe," Devi said. "Good luck."

"What about you?" Nicholas asked. "What happens now?"

"To me?" Devi smiled. It was a gorgeous, devious smile. "I go back to being who I am. This wasn't my story, it was yours."

Nicholas stopped walking. "And who are you?"

Devi kissed his cheek, then left him, saying only, "More than I seem."

ABOUT JOHN URBANCIK

John Urbancik has enjoyed magic since childhood. Though he claims not to be a magician himself, he has been accused of being a wizard.

In addition to books of poetry and a nonfiction book based on his podcast *Inkstains*, Urbancik has written books like the *DarkWalker* series, *Stale Reality* (also available in Russian), *Choose Your Doom*, and *The Night Carnival*.

Born on a small island in the northeast United States known as Manhattan, and having lived in places as far away as Madrid and Sydney, he is currently sequestered in an undisclosed location in the woods of Pennsylvania near the Susquehanna River.

9 781621 053316